From the top of the highest mountain to the ocean deeps, from the icy polar wastes to the burning heat of the deserts, the Earth has enormous variety. This book tells the fascinating story of the planet on which we live.

Acknowledgment:
The publishers would like to thank Wendy Body for acting as reading level consultant.

Photographic credits:
Page 41, Cameron Balloons; pages 13 (bottom), 14, 30, 35 (2) and 36, J. Allan Cash; page 13 (top), Dr A. J. Crosbie; pages 11 and 28, Robert Harding Picture Library; page 34, Dr N. Hulton; page 31 (top right), Dr T. Jennings (author); page 31 (top left) and back cover, G. Morris; page 37, Dr Ian Morrison; pages 19 and 29, Popperfoto. Drawing on page 40 by Robin Davies; drawings on pages 10 and 41 by Mick Usher. Cover by John Dillow.

Designed by Anne Matthews.

British Library Cataloguing in Publication Data

Jennings, Terry, *1938-*
    The earth.
    1. Earth
    I. Title   II. Cook, David
    550
    ISBN 0-7214-1228-9

First edition

Published by Ladybird Books Ltd Loughborough Leicestershire UK
Ladybird Books Inc Auburn Maine 04210 USA

Printed in England (3)

The Earth

written by TERRY JENNINGS
illustrated by DAVID COOK

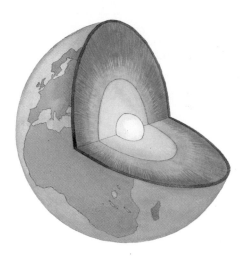

Ladybird Books

The Earth

The Earth we live on is like a huge ball, spinning in space.

When you stand on the ground you can't see what shape the Earth is. But if you were an astronaut in a spacecraft you would see that the Earth is round.

The **Equator** is an imaginary line that divides the Earth into two equal halves. The opposite ends of the Earth are called the Poles.

The bottom half of the Earth is called the southern hemisphere.

The top half of the Earth is called the northern hemisphere.

North Pole

Equator

South Pole

Day and night

Our Earth is spinning all the time, like a giant top. It takes twenty four hours (one day) to make one complete turn.

The Sun is much bigger than the Earth. It doesn't look it because it is so far away.

The Moon is much nearer to us, and is smaller than the Earth.

The Sun shines on one half of the Earth at a time. There, it is daytime. The other half of the Earth is in shadow. There, it is night.

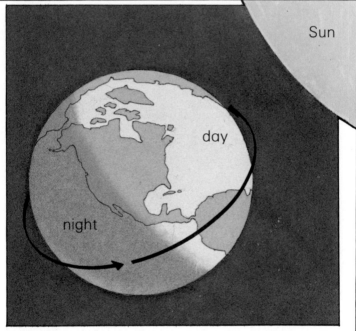

Sun

day

night

Sunlight travels in straight lines. It can't go round corners, so there are always dark shadows behind things that stand in its way.

The seasons

Not only does the Earth spin like a top, it also moves round the Sun. The Earth takes one year to go completely round the Sun.

In June the North Pole is tilted towards the Sun.

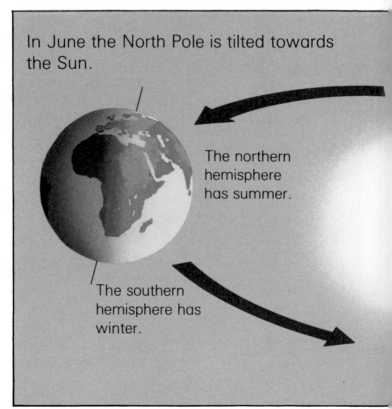

The northern hemisphere has summer.

The southern hemisphere has winter.

The Earth is slightly tilted. As it moves round the Sun, different parts of the Earth are tilted towards the Sun. This is what gives us the **seasons**.

In December the Earth is on the opposite side of the Sun. The North Pole is tilted away from the Sun.

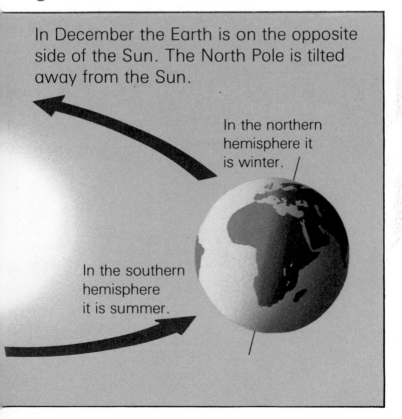

In the northern hemisphere it is winter.

In the southern hemisphere it is summer.

Moving air

The air around us is always moving, helping to spread the Sun's heat round the world. Moving air is called *wind*. Together with sunlight and water, it is one of the main ingredients in the world's **weather**.

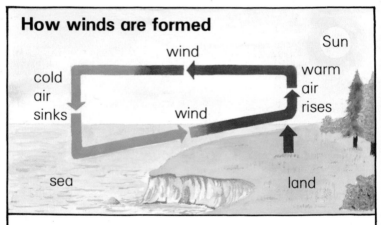

How winds are formed

Sun

wind

cold air sinks

warm air rises

wind

sea

land

The Sun warms up the air and the land. The warm air rises. Cold air then rushes in to take its place.

A hurricane in Sri Lanka

The strongest winds of all are called
hurricanes. These happen in hot sea
areas such as the Caribbean. The wind
can reach speeds of 300 km per hour,
destroying houses and crops in its path.

Beaufort Scale of Wind Speeds			
Force	Strength	Speed (kph)	Effect
0	Calm	0 – 1	
3	Gentle Breeze	20	
6	Strong Breeze	50	
8	Gale	75	
10	Storm	100 +	

Climate

The pattern of the weather in a particular place is called its **climate**.

Different parts of the world have different climates. The three main types of climate are *tropical* (hot and wet), *polar* (cold and icy) and *temperate* (mild).

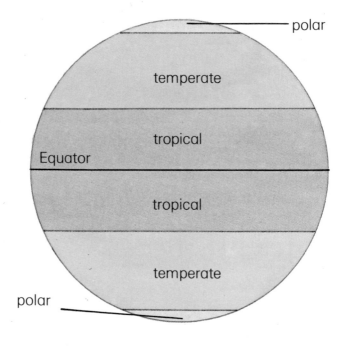

polar

temperate

tropical

Equator

tropical

temperate

polar

The hottest places are around the middle of the Earth, near the Equator. This is because the Equator never tilts away from the Sun. These places may also be very wet.

A rainforest in ▶ Papua New Guinea

Mount Kilimanjaro, Tanzania, Africa▼

The higher you go, the colder it gets. Some high mountains, even in warm places, always have snow at their tops.

13

The deserts

Deserts cover about one third of the Earth's land. Some are cold and dry, but most are the hottest and driest places in the world. The Sahara, in North Africa, is the world's largest desert. It covers about 7,700,000 sq km. This is about one third of Africa.

Cacti grow in some deserts. They are able to survive because they can store water in their thick, waxy stems.

A Mexican Cardon cactus

Some deserts are covered with rocks and pebbles, others with sand. Sandy deserts are shaped by the wind. It blows the sand into huge piles called sand dunes. The highest sand dunes are in the Sahara Desert. They are over 400 m high.

Camels are often used as transport in the desert. They can go for days without food or water.

The Poles

The Poles lie at the top and bottom of the Earth. The area round the *North Pole* is called the Arctic. There is no land here, just a huge floating sheet of ice. The area round the *South Pole* is called the Antarctic. The land here is covered with ice, up to 4 km thick in places.

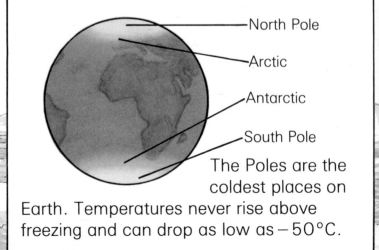

North Pole

Arctic

Antarctic

South Pole

The Poles are the coldest places on Earth. Temperatures never rise above freezing and can drop as low as −50°C.

Icebergs are huge chunks of ice that float in the sea round the Poles. Only about one ninth of an iceberg shows above the water, so ships have to be very careful to avoid them.

In spite of the cold, polar bears and seals live in the Arctic. They have thick layers of fat under their skin to protect them from the cold. At the other end of the world, penguins live happily in the Antarctic.

Oceans and seas

Nearly three quarters of the Earth is covered by water. Most of this is the salty water of the five **oceans** – the Pacific, the Atlantic, the Indian, the Arctic and the Antarctic.

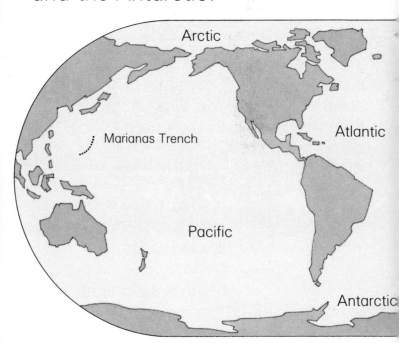

The Pacific is the largest ocean. The Marianas Trench in the Pacific Ocean is the deepest point on Earth. It is 11,033 m below sea level. The water here is pitch black and very cold.

The bathyscape *Trieste*

Indian

In 1960 the crew of the bathyscape *Trieste* dived almost to the bottom of the Marianas Trench. (A bathyscape is a type of small submarine.)

Most of the salt in sea water comes from rocks on land. Rain washes the salt out of the rocks and rivers carry it to the sea.

Lakes and rivers: fresh water

Most lakes and all rivers are filled with fresh water. This falls

1 Near its start, or *source*, a river flows straight and fast. It wears away the land and makes a *valley*.

Lakes form when water fills up hollows in the ground. Many of these hollows were scraped out by ice thousands of years ago.

as rain or snow and has no salt in it. Rivers start as small streams in hills and mountains. As the streams flow downhill, they join together to form rivers, which flow towards the sea.

2 Farther on, the river becomes slower and wider. It twists and turns around hard rocks. These twists are called *meanders*.

3 The place where the river reaches the sea is called the *mouth*. Here the river sets down much of the mud and rocks it has picked up.

The water cycle

The Earth has only a limited supply of water, which is used over and over again. The way this happens is called the **water cycle**.

1 As the Sun shines on oceans, lakes and rivers, the Sun's heat turns the water into invisible **water vapour**. This rises into the air.

2 As the water vapour rises, it cools and turns back into tiny droplets of water. These form clouds.

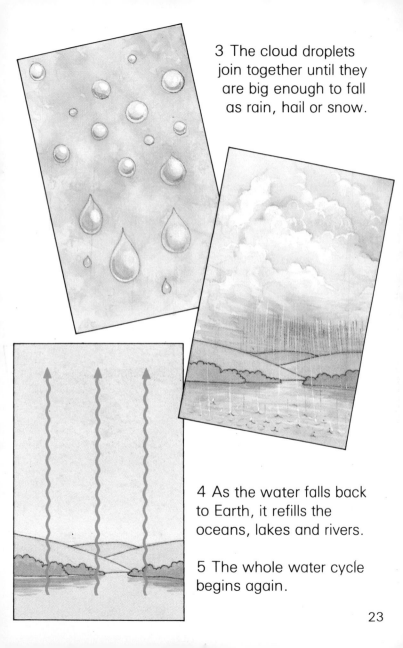

3 The cloud droplets join together until they are big enough to fall as rain, hail or snow.

4 As the water falls back to Earth, it refills the oceans, lakes and rivers.

5 The whole water cycle begins again.

23

Inside the Earth

This is what the Earth would look like if we cut it open.

The hard top layer is called the *crust*.

Under the crust is a layer of semi-liquid rock. This is called the *mantle*.

The centre of the Earth is called the *core*. The outer part is made of hot, liquid metals. It is about 2,000 km thick.

The inner part of the core is a ball of very hot metal. It is about 2,400 km across.

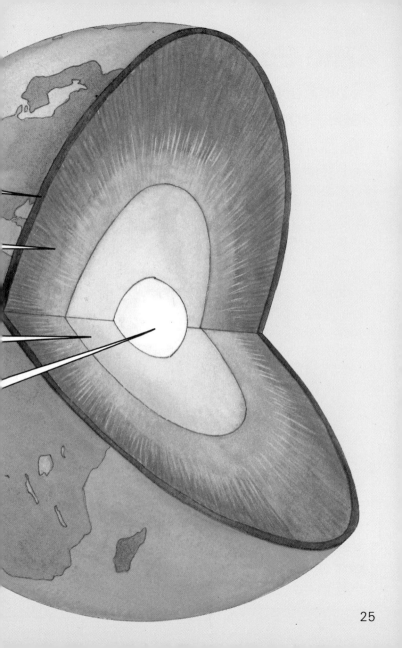

The Earth's crust

The Earth's crust is made of solid rock which can be up to 40 km thick in places. The part of the crust we can see is split

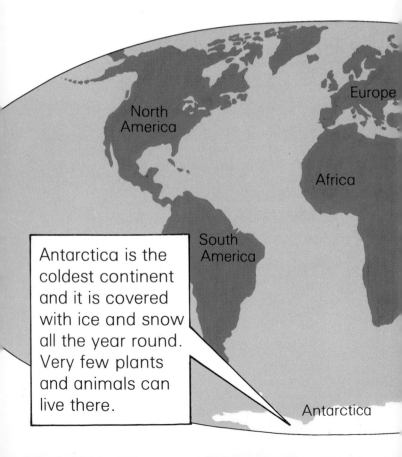

North America

Europe

Africa

South America

Antarctica is the coldest continent and it is covered with ice and snow all the year round. Very few plants and animals can live there.

Antarctica

into seven huge pieces of land, called **continents**. These are North America, South America, Europe, Africa, Asia, Australia and Antarctica.

Asia is the biggest continent and has the most people. Three fifths of all the people in the world live in Asia.

Asia

Australia

Australia is the smallest continent.

Earthquakes

There are cracks in the Earth's crust called *fault lines*. If the pieces of land on either side of a fault line crash into each other or jerk apart, the ground trembles. This is an *earthquake*. During

Earthquake in Mexico City, 1985

Some earthquakes cause terrible damage. In just a few minutes they can destroy whole cities, killing thousands of people.

an earthquake, huge cracks may appear in the ground, swallowing up buildings, cars and even people.

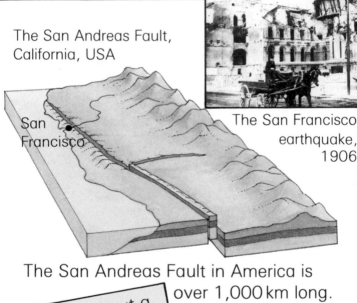

The San Andreas Fault, California, USA

San Francisco

The San Francisco earthquake, 1906

The San Andreas Fault in America is over 1,000 km long. The city of San Francisco lies on the fault line. There was a huge earthquake there in 1906, and another in 1989.

There are about a million earthquakes every year. Many happen under the sea, where the Earth's crust is very thin.

Mountains

Some parts of the Earth's surface are flat, but in other places there are high mountains.

Mount Everest in the Himalayas is the highest mountain on Earth. It is 8,848 m high.

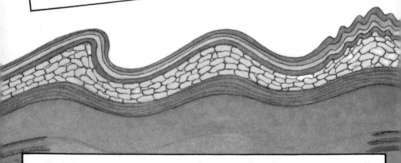

Fold mountains are formed when parts of the Earth's crust collide and push up huge layers of rock. The Himalayas, the Alps and the Andes are fold mountains.

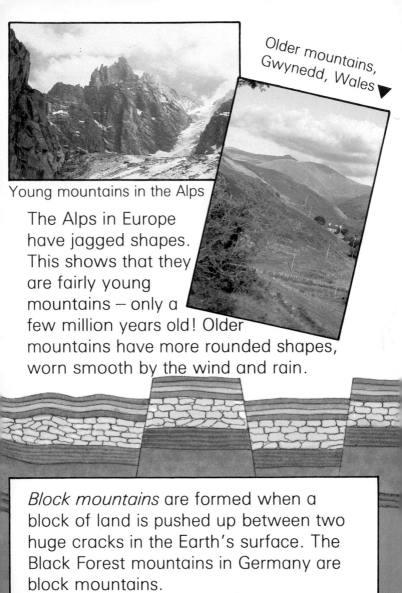

Older mountains, Gwynedd, Wales ▼

Young mountains in the Alps

The Alps in Europe have jagged shapes. This shows that they are fairly young mountains – only a few million years old! Older mountains have more rounded shapes, worn smooth by the wind and rain.

Block mountains are formed when a block of land is pushed up between two huge cracks in the Earth's surface. The Black Forest mountains in Germany are block mountains.

Volcanoes

Volcanoes erupt when pockets of hot, liquid rock inside the Earth burst up through cracks in the crust. The liquid rock is called *lava*. It cools and hardens as it flows and sometimes it forms a high, cone-shaped mountain. The force of the eruption may also throw clouds of gas, dust and rocks high into the air.

In 1883 Krakatoa in Indonesia erupted with the loudest bang ever. It could be heard nearly 5,000 km away in Australia.

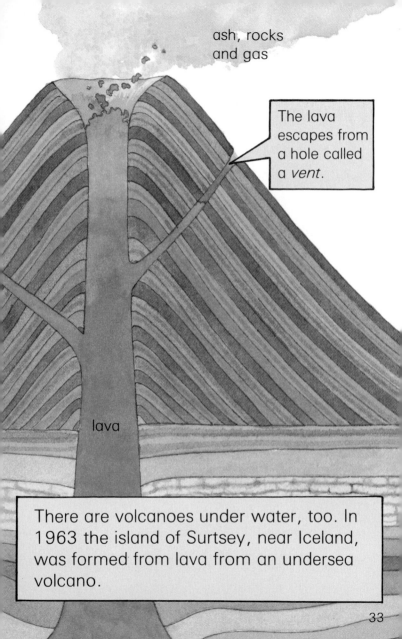

ash, rocks and gas

The lava escapes from a hole called a *vent*.

lava

There are volcanoes under water, too. In 1963 the island of Surtsey, near Iceland, was formed from lava from an undersea volcano.

Islands

Islands are pieces of land surrounded by water. Islands are formed in many different ways. Some are the tips of underwater mountains or volcanoes. Some are made of **coral**. Others were once part of continents and split off millions of years ago.

Greenland

Greenland is the world's largest island. It is nearly four times bigger than France.

The island of Madagascar was once part of the continent of Africa. Because it has been separate for so long, Madagascar has many animals and plants found nowhere else on Earth.

a lemur

The islands of Hawaii are the tips of underwater volcanoes.

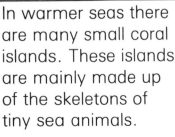

In warmer seas there are many small coral islands. These islands are mainly made up of the skeletons of tiny sea animals.

Great Barrier Reef, Australia

Wearing away the land

The Earth's surface is always being worn away by wind, rain and frost. Hot days and cold nights weaken rocks so that they crack. Plants grow in the cracks and widen them. And rivers wear away the land as they flow over it.

Tassili n'Ajjer

In the desert, sand blown by the wind wears rocks into unusual shapes. The huge cliffs of Tassili n'Ajjer in the Sahara Desert were formed in this way.

In cold places rivers of ice called *glaciers* slowly wear away the rocks they flow over.

This is a glacier in Iceland. The ice scrapes away the land, carrying pieces of rock with it.

Mountains are worn down very slowly. It takes about 1,000 years to wear down 8 cm.

Natural resources

The Earth supplies us with many fuels and other materials. These are called *natural resources*.

We use oil, gas and coal from deep under the ground to make heat and light.

Cars, machines and jewellery are made from metals found in rocks in the Earth's crust.

Oil, gas and coal are **fossil fuels**. They were formed millions of years ago from the bodies of animals and plants.

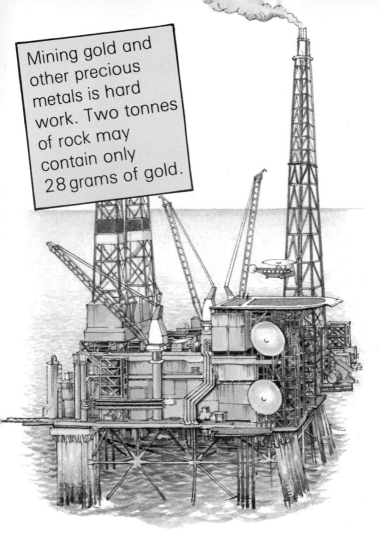

Mining gold and other precious metals is hard work. Two tonnes of rock may contain only 28 grams of gold.

About one fifth of our oil comes from under the sea. Huge drills are used to make holes in the sea bed. Then the oil is pumped up.

The atmosphere

All round the Earth is a thick layer of air called the **atmosphere**. Part of the air is a gas called **oxygen**. People and animals must breathe oxygen to stay alive.

40,000 m

High altitude balloon 38,000 m

30,000 m

20,000 m

Jet aircraft

10,000 m

Helicopters

Birds

Highest building 443 m

THE STRATOSPHERE 50 km

Cirrus Cloud

Mount Everest (8848 m)

THE TROPOSPHERE 10 km

Cumulus Cloud

In sunlight, plants can make oxygen. Without plants, humans and other animals would soon use up all the oxygen in the air. Near the ground there is plenty of air. As you go higher and higher, there is less air.

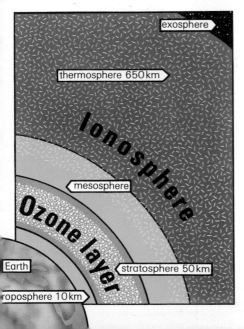

exosphere

thermosphere 650 km

Ionosphere

mesosphere

Ozone layer

Earth

stratosphere 50 km

troposphere 10 km

The pilots of hot air balloons that climb high into the atmosphere must carry oxygen so that they can breathe. High in the sky, there is no air at all. Then you are in **space**.

Changing the climate

The Earth's climate may be getting warmer. Smoke and fumes from factories, power stations and cars are collecting

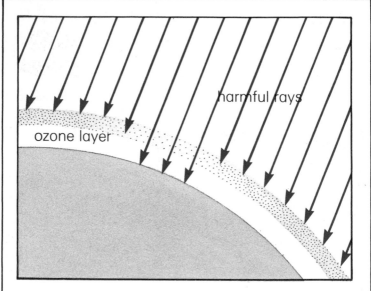

harmful rays

ozone layer

Gases called **CFCs** are also changing the climate by destroying the **ozone layer** round the Earth. This layer protects us from the Sun's harmful rays, which may damage our skin if they reach the Earth.

high in the sky and forming a blanket round the Earth. This blanket stops extra heat escaping from the Earth and makes the air warmer than usual. If the Earth gets too warm, the ice at the Poles may melt. This may make the seas rise and cover low-lying places.

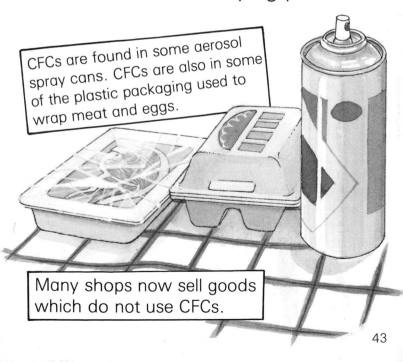

CFCs are found in some aerosol spray cans. CFCs are also in some of the plastic packaging used to wrap meat and eggs.

Many shops now sell goods which do not use CFCs.

Glossary

atmosphere The thick layer of air around the Earth.

CFCs This stands for chlorofluorocarbon gases, which are damaging the ozone layer.

climate The sort of weather a place usually gets.

continent One of the seven very large areas of land in the world.

coral A hard substance made up of the skeletons of tiny sea creatures.

Equator An imaginary line round the middle of the Earth.

fossil fuels Fuels such as coal, oil or natural gas, formed from the remains of plants and animals millions of years ago.

island A piece of land surrounded by water.

ocean One of the five great areas of salt water.

oxygen The gas in the air that all living things need to breathe in order to stay alive.

ozone layer The upper layer of the Earth's atmosphere containing ozone gas which blocks out some of the Sun's harmful rays.

seasons The division of the year into spring, summer, autumn and winter in temperate climates.

space All the places beyond the Earth's atmosphere.

volcano A crack in the Earth's surface formed when liquid rock, gases and ash burst through the crust.

water cycle The way in which water is used over and over again in nature.

water vapour The invisible gas formed when water is heated. Water vapour is always present in the air.

weather Rain, snow, fog, ice, wind, sunshine and other changes in the air.